DERELICTION OF DEVOTION

The Case of the Stolen Diamond

BUTTERS P.I.

RORI BLEU

ROSIE CHAPEL

First printing: 2025
ISBN: 978-1-7644985-0-0 (ebook)
ISBN: 978-1-7644985-1-7 (paperback)

Ulfire Pty. Ltd.
P.O. Box 1481
South Perth
WA 6951
Australia

Cover Design: Rebecca Norman
Images Courtesy: Canva and Deposit Photos
Designed in Canva using appropriate licences.

❀ Formatted with Vellum

DERELICTION OF DEVOTION

Butters P.I.

"Down these mean streets a man must go who is not himself mean, who is neither tarnished nor afraid.
The detective must be a complete man and a common man and yet an unusual man.
He must be, to use a rather weathered phrase, a man of honor—by instinct, by inevitability, without thought of it, and certainly without saying it.
He must be the best man in his world and a good enough man for any world."

The Simple Art of Murder
Raymond Chandler

CHAPTER ONE

1940 - San Francisco

The funny thing about life is you never know what fate has in store. Case in point, the opening of yours truly's private investigations office at the onset of the Second World War.

It's one thing for the average schmuck to hang a shingle and call himself a gumshoe, but when a disgraced member of the San Francisco Homicide Squad does it, the shadiest of clientele crawl out of the woodwork and there is no lack of them in the City by the Bay.

Friday September 13th, 1940, started out pretty much like any other day… in the midst of a worldwide strife. Buckingham Palace, King George VI's London home was damaged by German bombs during the air raids known as the Blitz.

In Africa, Italian troops under Marshal Graziani attacked Egypt in an effort to drive the British out.

In my little corner of the world, Friday the 13th marked a significant, and unlucky, turning point in my life.

It all began when my business partner, and live-in lover, Stella Fitzhugh, decided that because she had few hours to spare, it was high time she caught up on the never-ending paperwork. From the moment we offered our… well, mine mostly… services to the city, our caseload was unrelenting.

Cheating spouses, missing people, minor thefts and such-like, along with any and all offences the various police departments deemed unworthy of investigation, were dropped at our doorstep. All had to be solved and invoiced.

Especially since we had bills to pay.

On this particular morning, while Stella was buried in invoicing, I was following some slime-ball around the city who was bedding any woman naive enough to fall for his BS about being widowed. Meanwhile, his stay-at-home wife nursed a baby bottle of scotch and paid twenty-five dollars a day plus expenses to collect evidence for the sole purpose of saving her marriage.

I may judge people's motivation for hiring us, but as long as their checks clear, I don't judge them… much.

The problem with this case were the numerous and protracted intervals I was required to be out of the office, leaving me less time with my bedmate.

…but I digress…

Whoever said peeping through keyholes for a living… figuratively speaking, of course… wasn't arduous, never walked in the shoes of a private investigator whose client demanded immediate proof that her husband was having an affair.

Exhausted, I dragged myself back to the office around ten in the evening, surprised to see Stella's silhouette through the frosted glass of the door.

I turned the knob to find it locked, relieved that, even when she knows I'm on my way, she has the foresight to consider her safety when alone in the office after dark.

Digging out my keys, I unlocked the door and went in to find Stella staring at the entrance blankly. She was unnervingly still.

Concerned, I crossed the floor. As though the sound of my approach broke a spell, she refocused, and folded her arms, barking, "Take one more step, Jacob Butterfield, and I'll give you a demonstration of how much better my aim has become on that fancy nickel-plated pistol you bought me out of petty cash, since you shelled out for shooting lessons."

"How very generous of me." I grinned, trying to break whatever tension had suddenly filled the room... and our relationship.

"Don't waste your breath humoring me. Just park your butt in that chair." She jabbed a finger at the one at the other side of her desk.

My smile faded and I felt like a schoolboy being hauled in front of the principal for a misdemeanor I failed to recall.

"We need to talk," she said flatly. "Are you done with the philandering husband case, or do you need more time to comfort the poor distraught wife, while getting your jollies watching the man diddle his secretary?" Adding, facetiously, "Or have you decided to join in the fun?"

My forehead puckered into an uncomprehending frown. Stella knew I did not play around. I had hardly looked at another woman since our loose friendship, which occasionally included sex, had evolved into whatever this was.

"Stella, I don't know what you're talking about but, rest assured, everything will be wrapped up in the next day—"

"Wrong, Butterfield, you close that case tonight. Have a courier deliver the evidence, along with our final bill. If that doesn't satisfy her, she can sue us."

"I know Eleanor—"

"Eleanor? Oh, we are on a first name basis with the client?" her voice dripped with sarcasm.

"No..." I corrected quickly, "...Mrs. Peterson had some fresh information about her husband's extra-marital activities and where he conducts them."

"How much more does she need? Surely, given how *diligently* you have worked," I heard the snarky emphasis on diligently and the crease in my brow deepened at her insinuation, "she has enough dirt on him to win twenty divorce cases. This has gone way beyond what she hired us to do."

"Why the fit of the grumps, Stella? It's not like Rich Aunt Moneybags..." hopefully a certain board game company will forgive me for the feminization of their famed wealthy uncle in an attempt to diffuse the friction, "...has missed a payment has she?"

Annoyed, she countered, "No, but we have other cases that need your..." she amended, "...*our* attention."

She picked up a file and pushed it over the desk to me. A picture of an odd-looking diamond, torn from a book, slid out along with handwritten notes about its original discovery centuries ago, and its loss from a Flemish chateau during the last war.

"Looks like someone spent the day at the library," I teased lightly.

"For the money we are looking at for recovering that rock, you bet."

"How much?" I asked idly. Her reply prompted a shocked,

"Twenty-thousand dollars? Stella, who has that kind of dough? I take it this prospective client is not some minor royal fleeing a revolution?"

"Not that I'm aware."

"Then who?" I stared at her.

A delicate pink washed up her cheeks. "I don't know. His representative was tight lipped in that regard, but come on Jacob, we could use the money," she argued diffidently.

I couldn't refute that, and tried to keep an open mind, while unpleasant possibilities chased through my head.

Reading the paperwork, one detail nagged at me. "Recover? Says here, the diamond vanished at the end of the Great War, probably appropriated by a returning soldier, and hasn't been seen since."

"Let's just say, news of its loss is premature. Seems someone here in the States was able to acquire it."

"The non-royal," I said sarcastically, "who is willing to pay a handsome fee for finding an already found rock? Any chance it's the previous owners, assuming they are still alive?"

"I have no clue what happened to them," Stella huffed. "Have you even read my notes? It's the guy who bought it five or six years ago, but he doesn't want to be kept hanging until your adolescent infatuation with a millionaire's wife comes to an end."

Ignoring Stella's appraisal of my business dealings with Eleanor Peterson, I returned to the matter at hand. "Let me get this straight. The guy who bought a stolen diamond wants us to recover it. From whom?"

"The thief."

It was all I could do not to slap my forehead.

"Okay, Stella, how about we start this conversation again."

CHAPTER TWO

Settling back in her chair, Stella composed herself. I recognized the signs and swallowed a groan. For someone succinct in most aspects of her life, when it came to recounting something out of the ordinary... *read lucrative...* she invariably opted for unabbreviated over abridged.

Yielding to the inevitable, I hid a yawn, steeled myself for a long night, and tried to concentrate.

I give you chapter and verse.

Earlier that day

The sunlight through the stained-glass arches atop the picture windows painted the floor with myriad rainbows. It was this embellishment which had clinched the deal for Stella when we were selecting an office, despite the questionable locality.

As she finished the weekly customer billing, the door to

the office creaked open to announce the arrival of a potential client.

Knowing I was out, and with no idea for how long, she did not bother to look up from the paperwork. Not in the right frame of mind to accept new business, she mumbled, "I am sorry you have wasted your time but—"

A chuckle, then, "Butter, huh?"

Reining in her irritation at the interruption, Stella lifted her head to see a man pointing at the partially stenciled sign on the door.

"Hey doll, your boss too poor to afford the whole of his name?" he asked with a cheesy grin, removing his hat to dip a cursory, and oddly formal, bow.

Instinctively, Stella rolled her eyes, not as quickly as usual, allowing her time to give the man the once-over.

Tall, heavy-set and, despite the smattering of gray at his temples, his slicked-back hair was a dark, russet red, making it difficult to determine his age. Immaculately dressed, his hand-tailored linen suit fitted him like a glove, save the, cleverly designed and scarcely noticeable, bulge under the left side of his jacket. Large enough to conceal a weapon in its holster, and detectable only to someone who has dealt with these types of characters.

Stella guessed he was packing a .45 automatic. *Was its size compensating for a perceived physical shortcoming?*

Her scrutiny complete and wondering how the visitor knew the name on the door was unfinished, Stella held his penetrating gaze. "I assure you, sir, *my partner and I* are experts in our chosen profession, and well paid as such, but due to the pending war, *we* decided to conserve paint on frivolous things, like adding the final touches to door decorations, in case it is needed.

"If you are done picking faults… and, given the length of our tenancy, unlikely to be representative of the neighborhood welcome wagon, nor are you a cop... perhaps you could get to the purpose of your vis—"

"Yeah, yeah, doll," the lug cut Stella off. "My employer sent me to talk to your boss. I have a job for him."

That answered one question.

"My partner," Stella reiterated loftily, "is following a lead, meaning, you're stuck flapping your gums at me."

What she said next was more direct order than polite invitation, "Have a seat, and how about you introduce yourself properly."

The stranger paused as though considering a smart comeback, then thought better of it, and sank into one of the office chairs Stella had acquired from the building manager when we took occupancy. He settled his hat on his lap, then stared at the woman across the battered, yet polished desk.

Stella noted his craggy features, chewing the inside of her lip, as she assessed him. He was no oil painting, but there was something about him... an aura of danger, an underlying hint of savagery. As alarming as it was inexplicably attractive. *He's the type I'd normally drop my panties for... before Jacob that is.*

The man opposite smiled, as though reading her thoughts, and ran a meaty hand through his hair, introducing himself at long last, "The name is Russo, Carmine Russo."

"Nice to meet you, Mister Russo. How may our agency be of service?"

Russo rubbed the scruffy stubble hugging his chin, "Returning the favor of an introduction would be a start. Are you by any chance, Mrs. Butterfield?"

"Hardly," Stella was not quite able to mask her disappointment. "As I told you already, buster—"

"Mister Russo... or Carmine would be better."

"Whatever. I am Mr. Butterfield's partner. My name is Stella, Stella Fitzhugh." She opened a drawer, withdrew her

PI badge — recently minted at my suggestion because her involvement far exceeded that of office manager — and flashed it theatrically. She had yet to use it, but this wiseacre's assumption, her role was inconsequential, like a secretary or worse, a wife was galling.

"Shiny," was his flippant reply.

Dropping it back into her drawer, she demanded, "Since we're past the pleasantries, why are you here?"

Russo sent her a dubious look, which stated as loudly as though he had spoken, *I would be more comfortable speaking with the man of the house.*

Stella lifted her chin. "Mr. Russo, anything you have to tell Jacob, you can tell me. If you prefer to wait until he returns, I can give you a blanket and pillow, so you can make yourself comfortable in the stairwell."

Russo held up a palm in submission. "All right, all right, I surrender."

"Fine, then let's be adults. Why are you here?"

"As I said, my employer—"

"Who is?" Stella interrupted abruptly.

"None of your concern, at present," Russo retorted. "I guarantee he is wealthy enough to cover this office's expenses. Hell, he could buy you out and not flinch."

"Okay, so what does this mystery man want?"

"He has had something precious, of a personal nature, taken from him."

"Why doesn't he go to the San Francisco Robbery Division? I hear they do a halfway decent job of recovering stolen items."

"Let's just say he and the police do not walk on the same side of the street."

"Thank you, Mr. Russo, that's all I need to hear. We are a reputable agency and have no need to deal with the mob."

"Not even for a twenty-thousand-dollar finder's fee?"

Stella cursed inwardly. Money was her Achilles' heel and, to be fair, for that amount, more than her heel was interested.

"Okay, Mister Russo, you have ten minutes of my time."

Carmine Russo began his tale.

"After the armistice was signed at the end of the Great War, and the Allied soldiers began the slow and often convoluted process of being demobbed, a certain unit was billeted in a crumbling old mansion on the Flemish border."

"A chateau," Stella corrected a trifle imperiously, her nose crinkling at the man's lack of knowledge.

He brushed aside her interruption. "Name doesn't matter. What does matter is that during the night a handful of them decided to explore. For the duration of the conflict, the *chateau* was commandeered by the Allies as a hospital, but the family had stored their belongings in the attics for safe-keeping."

"*Safekeeping?*" Stella expostulated. "In the middle of a war? Clearly the nobility believed their possessions were sacrosanct."

Russo chuckled wryly. "Clearly, they did not reckon on a pack of war-weary soldiers descending on their home whose greed trumped common sense. Method of removal aside and, no I am not condoning theft, but that cannot be undone..."

"The items could be returned to their rightful owner," Stella pointed out scathingly.

"If you might let me speak." He glared.

Quelling the urge to roll her eyes again, Stella made an apologetic sweep of her hand, indicating she was happy for him to continue.

"Anyway..." he drew out the word, "...according to my boss—"

"Your Mafioso Don—" Stella could not help reigniting their verbal swordplay.

"If you don't mind, doll, please shuddup and let me finish my story. By the way, you owe me two minutes for interrupting. As I was saying, they purloined some valuable goods. Art, small sculptures, jewelry, anything which could be stuffed into their knapsacks."

"So, it's knick-knacks. Trinkets," Stella interposed indifferently, losing interest.

Russo continued as though she had not spoken. "One of the more enterprising fellows had rifled through a set of trunks where he unearthed, hidden among some fancy clothing and whatnot, a handful of diamonds."

That caught Stella's attention, and she sat up straight.

"D-Diamonds?" she choked out incredulously.

"Nothing unusual about that, apparently. According to my boss, precious stones, as well as gold, acted as currency, and that many European aristocrats stripped the gems from their tiaras and crowns so they had a way to negotiate should it prove necessary."

Presumably, out of harm's way, Stella mused, suppressing a shudder at the notion of your life depending on someone else's desire for a ruby. Before a vision of sparkling rocks distracted her completely, she dragged her focus back to Russo.

"I have no clue how they smuggled out their ill-gotten gains, but I doubt the powers that be looked too hard. Suffice it to say, they escaped with their booty and brought it back to the States. I have no clue what happened to most of it. Perhaps the soldiers kept what they had stolen as souvenirs, justifying it as payment for enduring four years of horror." Russo shrugged.

"I only know about this through my boss, by the way. The government, not to mention the military, frowns upon the unauthorized removal of property. There were whispers over the years, but people wanted to forget about the war, so didn't delve too deeply into any of the reports. What the eye didn't see the heart couldn't grieve over.

"Then a few years ago, rumors began to percolate about a piece from the so-called Flemish collection, being for sale. My boss got wind of it through confidential channels…"

"You mean the black market?" Stella was unable to prevent a sneer.

Russo cut her off with an irritated look. "…and approached the seller by means of a third party. Described as a unique diamond, it was without provenance, obviously, but its quality suggested it originated from one of the Boer mines in the Transvaal, a province of the Union of South Africa," he clarified, "or perhaps Australia.

"Once he saw it, my boss, who is not an idiot when it comes to diamonds, agreed to pay the asking price, didn't even try to bargain."

"What makes this one so special?"

"From what I understand, diamonds with flaws are next to worthless, but this one was different. The flaw resembled a blue heart set in the stone, and had earned the nickname the Heart of Ice."

Her interest piqued, Stella felt her neutral expression slip briefly and, adept at reading people, imagined him thinking, *It's true what they say about dames and diamonds.*

Paying no heed to the faintly sardonic twist of his lips, she asked, "Then what happened?"

"Now the proud owner of the diamond, he puts it in his safe only showing it off to trusted friends, and rarely at that. Then two weeks ago, he moved house. Lo and behold, when he checks his safe, the gem has vanished, along with a decent amount of money and a handful of important documents."

"Did anyone question the people working for the moving company?"

"Yeah, every last one was interrogated but no one 'fessed up."

Stella understood by his tone that *interrogated* meant with extreme malice. "And the police?" she pressed and stifled a grin, keenly aware how unsympathetic this institution were to the likes of Mr. Russo and his employer.

"As I said before, the inclination of SFPD's finest to help my boss is less than zero, hence my presence in the office of a discredited former homicide detective."

"All I'm prepared to say," Stella replied gruffly trying to ignore the slur, "is that I shall discuss the case with Jacob, and we will get back to you. Do you have a contact number where I can reach you, which isn't Central Booking?"

Russo chuckled at her impudence and tossed a business card on the desk. "You can find me here."

Standing, he tipped his hat to her, and then placed it on his head. "I look forward to hearing from Mr. Butterfield or, better yet, *you*, Miss Fitzhugh."

He walked out, leaving Stella staring after him, mouth agape.

CHAPTER THREE

It was past midnight by the time we had finished perusing Stella's comprehensive notes. I was impressed by her aptitude for ferreting out all manner of minutiae, which could easily be dismissed as immaterial but were, in fact, relevant, from the books and newspapers in the library.

She had also taken the time to include notes relating to the disappearance of something called the Florentine Diamond, which had vanished in eerily similar circumstances.

The pale-yellow gem, of Indian origin, had passed through many illustrious hands since its discovery, from dukes to popes, from the Medicis to the Hapsburgs. Sometime in 1918 when its then owner, Emperor Charles I of Austria was in exile, it was stolen and, purportedly, taken to South America, before finding its way to the States in the 1920s, where it was believed to have been re-cut and sold.

While the parallels could not be ignored, the diamond described by our potential new client ruled out the possibility it was an off cut of the Florentine; the colors did not match. That said, Stella's initiative in tracking down this article highlighted the challenges of recovering a stone once in the hands of unscrupulous dealers who would either sell it to a private collector or carve it up until it was unrecognizable.

It dawned on me that I had once again, for my sins, underestimated my partner's ability. Stella was the one who had driven our venture from fledgling idea to official organization, her range of skills… attested to by her PI badge… indisputable and indispensable. Despite this, I had not shaken my tendency to view her as little more than an airheaded cocktail waitress in pursuit of the next sucker and their crinkled greenback.

Neither had I pressed her for details about her life before we met, something any former cop and current private investigator worth a damn would be a fool to neglect. Then again, anyone else would have probably kicked her ass out of their apartment after our long ago, supposed to be, one-night stand.

Tired, and conceding there was nothing we could do tonight, we tidied up and closed the office. As we descended the stairs to the street, and relieved the hours spent discussing the diamond heist had taken her mind off the Peterson affair, I said, "I know where there is an all-night diner. Care for a bite?"

"Is it another of your women of ill repute hangouts?"

Two faces from the past teased my subconscious, causing me to grimace. Fortunately, Stella was digging through her purse for one of her noxious Turkish cigarettes and missed it.

Even after all this time, Mae and June's murdered souls had the power to reach out from their graves in Colma. I forced them back, and summoned up a chuckle.

"Nah. Too many *honest* cops eat there."

"Is that still possible?" Stella replied with a crooked smile.

"Well, at least enough to fill a corner booth."

We climbed into my DeSoto Six and I drove towards the Financial District.

To the uninitiated, Ruby's... tucked along Front Street... was the epitome of a greasy spoon, whose stubborn resistance to change was why we liked it so much. The patrons, most of whom had been coming since they could walk, did not want some trendy, know-it-all tycoon swooping in to buy the diner then destroy its character by deciding it needed beautifying, or whatever crap term they used to make things sound attractive to the nouveau-riche.

The tables were clean... after a fashion, the food... mouthwatering, unless the cook was having one of his tantrums, and the clientele... unremarkable. A no-questions asked place, as long as you paid your bill and kept a civil tongue in your head. It had been one of SFPD's watering holes of choice for decades.

With any luck, we might actually find an honest officer in there.

The bell above the door chimed our entrance and when we stepped over the threshold, the cacophony of multiple conversations lapsed into an uncomfortable silence, all eyes on us.

We headed to the counter, hearing one of the beat cops in the cheap seats growl snidely, "Opal, do I need to call the health department and report you for letting scum pollute your fine establishment?"

Before I could put him in his place with my cutting repartee, a voice, like nails on a chalkboard, screeched, "All right, O'Reilly, button it."

My attention shifted from the patrolman to the woman parked behind the counter, hands on hips, a well-worn bandana binding up her mop of dark chestnut hair, effectively hiding the streaks of silver threading her temples.

Opal, the aforementioned Ruby's daughter, had worked alongside, then taken over from her mother when the latter developed arthritis.

That is not to say Ruby had relinquished complete control and often perched like an aging crow in one of the booths, monitoring proceedings. Thankfully, tonight she had not seen fit to grace the diner with her beady-eyed presence.

I loved Ruby but, boy, she saw more than you wanted her to.

With a nod, Opal beckoned us to join her on the stools tucked under the brand spanking new, red Formica.

"Evening, Opal." Smiling, I greeted my second favorite fast food proprietor, losing out to Clara only because of the distance between this place and my apartment.

"Butterfield. Long time no see. Usual?" she asked, which, despite it being months since my last visit, spoke of how frequently I used to eat here, especially when I worked the graveyard shift as a homicide detective.

"Thanks, Opal." Surprised she remembered. "Stella?" I raised a brow at my partner who was studying the board on the wall above the back of the counter.

"What's your usual?" she muttered.

"Fried chicken, scalloped potatoes, and a cup of the worst mud anybody dares to call coffee."

Stella looked at Opal. "Same for me too, please."

"Coming up…" Opal grinned, "…and, deary, I'll make sure you get coffee from a fresh pot, unlike that mug next to you."

Stella laughed as Opal yelled the order through to the cook.

Our meal arrived and we ate without talking but, while

we drank the not even close to mud-tasting coffee, we resumed our earlier conversation.

"Our biggest problem in trying to identify the perp, is that even a half-brained idiot will not be advertising the theft," I ruminated out loud.

"True," Stella agreed. "The diamond is entirely too distinctive. What we need is someone who knows someone who knows someone."

Her suggestion caused an involuntary glance over my shoulder at my erstwhile colleagues who had for the moment, at least, forgotten my presence.

Most I discounted. In the main because I did not trust them, but also because they would not recognize the phrase *button your lip* if it slapped them square across the jaw with a fish wrapped around a baseball bat.

Then I spotted Frank Gilbert... Gil to friends and enemies alike. Tall, broad, dark-haired, and dark eyed, Gil cultivated the veneer of a hard-faced no-nonsense cop. Which he was... to anyone who broke the law. Away from the office, he was a private man who loved his wife and kids, enjoyed fishing, and tinkering with cars.

He was fiercely loyal, but piss him off or threaten anyone he cared about, and he became a formidable foe.

We met the first day I was assigned to the squad, and had been friends ever since. He was about the only cop who stood by me when the shit hit the fan and, although we did not get together as often, chiefly because I did not want to put him in an awkward position with the rest of the depart-ment, we had kept in touch.

It's conceivable his association with me precipitated his transfer from Homicide to Robbery, but he knows how the game is played and never held it against me. He focused on doing his job, and providing for his family.

Gil, more so than my former partner, Louis Mazzetti, was

the one we could rely on to dredge up any intelligence. He had a longer string of informants working under his thumb than Mazzetti had bordellos and hookers flinging him bribe money.

If anyone could get the information we needed, however nebulous, about the theft without leaking like a bald Firestone tire it was Gil.

I was mulling over how to approach him when Stella did it for me.

"Gil? Is that you Gil?" she trilled brightly, waving enthusiastically.

My jaw dropped. *How did she know Gil?*

CHAPTER FOUR

My brain went into overdrive, and I strove to quash the flurry of unwelcome scenarios crowding my head, as Gil said something to his buddies, and strolled over to where we were sitting.

He greeted Stella with a warm hug.

My eyes were on stalks.

"Stella, how lovely to see you again," he spoke with old world charm, his smile sincere and in no way indicative of a past intimacy.

"Errr." Corralling my wits, I coaxed my recalcitrant thoughts back to the conversation. "Gil, great to see you. How do you two know each other?" I swung a vaguely accusatory gaze between them.

"Stella introduced me to my wife," Gil elaborated.

I do not think I could have been any more shocked. "Y-Your wife," I croaked.

"Is my cousin," Stella patted my hand, "with a generous heart, and enough money to bail my butt out of jail… should the occasion arise." She grinned wickedly at my stupefaction. "Close your mouth, Jacob dear, you look like a stranded cod."

While Stella being bailed out of jail or her insult ought to have been my overriding concerns… neither was what I took from that verbal back and forth.

"You have a cousin?" I stammered, unable to stop the question spilling out, my earlier thoughts returning with a vengeance.

"I have three, actually… plus an aunt and uncle who live in Bernal Heights. Had you shown the slightest interest, I would have told you," Stella replied lightly, "and ol' Gil here helped Hattie get me out of a sticky situation."

Collecting myself, I dipped my head with deliberate formality. "I have been sorely remiss. My apologies."

Stella chuckled wryly. "Forget it, Butters. Being meek does not become you. I don't know much about your family either."

She patted the swivel stool next to her for Gil to join us, an invitation he did not need repeating. We made small talk for a few moments, then Stella got to the point.

"Gil, might I ask a huge favor?"

"Depends. Is this going to end up with my neck on the line?" He winked at her, then narrowed his eyes at me, as though I was the source of all the world's ills.

I made a conciliarity gesture and waited for Stella to continue. This was her case.

My deference did not appear to assuage Gil's suspicions. In fact, his demeanor underwent a subtle change, his tone becoming a shade censorious. "What has this bum…" he prodded my shoulder, "…got you involved in? You know what the judge said about getting into more trouble… locked away until you're old and gray."

"No, no, Gil. It's nothing like that. A case with a large payoff has fallen into our laps, and we need your help," Stella mollified.

Unconvinced, Gil pursed his lips. "Go on, but tread lightly, cousin. You may be family, but I'm still a cop."

Careful not to name names, Stella provided a concise account of Carmine Russo's visit.

"Okay, let me get this straight. You want me to see whether there's any intel on this theft?" Gil asked in utter disbelief.

"Anything is more than we have now," Stella sighed.

"It's safe to assume this marble your client has… or had… in his possession is wartime contraband. Ya know the government doesn't approve of stolen antiquities being smuggled into the States. In fact, Mr. Hoover gets downright pissy about it," Gil reproved.

"Pissy?" Stella howled with mirth, attracting disgruntled looks from the cops trying to finish their meal before returning to their beats. "You have been married to Hattie for too long. Besides, there were no legalities at the time, it fell into the jurisdiction of finders keepers, and what J. Edgar doesn't know can't hurt us."

Gil whistled through his teeth at Stella's flippant reply, especially given his job. "Okay, cuz, I'll see what I can dredge up, and Butterfield." He shot me a cutting look. "See nothing happens to her, or *you'll* be the one answering to Hattie."

We made it home sometime after two in the morning. Stella was so quiet in the car that, at one point, I suspected she had fallen asleep. Only the glowing embers of her cigarette told me otherwise.

Entering the building, we climbed the stairs. The blare of a radio through the door of Esmeralda Harper's apartment, inferred our landlady had probably dozed off in her usual drunken stupor.

I felt partially responsible for bankrolling her drinking when she doubled my rent to cover Stella's presence... one of the reasons the two women did not get along. The second being something about what we did for a living being unsuitable for a proper lady.

Proper lady... I swallowed a snort. *If the old sot knew what the two of us got up to in the apartment above hers, she would know Stella was anything but ladylike. Then again, that she* had *overheard us, might explain her increased consumption.*

Her brows knitted, Stella shook her head at the disturbance and continued upwards. Reaching our apartment, she did not wait for me to be the gentleman. Unlocking the door, she walked in, dropped her hat and coat on the living room chair, and headed to the icebox for a beer.

"Wow," I drawled. "Yes, I would like a beer, thank you for asking?"

"Oh, I'm sorry. I thought your precious Eleanor would appear to serve your majesty."

I felt the beginnings of a headache. "For Christ's sake, Stella. We've been through this already. We're taking the diamond case, and I'll close the one on the Petersons."

"Oh, did we reach that conclusion? I don't remember you calling the courier."

"After ten at night? Come on," I argued... rationally, I thought. "I'll call Mrs. Peterson first thing in the morning. You're right, there's enough evidence for her to file for an incontestable divorce."

"Fine by me, as long as it's done."

Stella's agreement came too quickly.

"Why not come with me? You'll see everything is on the up and up."

"I shouldn't have to, Jacob, so I'll pass," Stella sniped

cattily. "Neither do I have any inclination to meet your current fling."

I cringed at her accusation as I grasped a bottle from the ice box. There was nothing between Eleanor and me. I had no desire to spend any longer in the company of the, outwardly at least, heartbroken wife, never mind bed her, but was at a loss as to how to persuade Stella of this fact.

Popping the cap off the beer, I took a swig. "I don't suppose we can call it a night and head to bed?"

She emptied her bottle and dropped it on the draining board with a clatter. "Absolutely, Butters. The couch is all yours." She smiled without humor, turned her back, stripped, and got into bed. Rolling away from me, she pulled up the covers around her shoulders.

Stupidly, I stared at her for a moment, then kicked off my shoes in her direction like a petulant child, stretched out on the sofa, and shut my eyes.

Sleep is an elusive mistress when your life is in turmoil.

It is amazing how not having a warm body next to you makes it hard to get a decent night's rest. I tossed and turned, freezing my butt off because I had not bothered to grab a blanket.

We might be hovering on the cusp of Fall... but I reckoned winter was clawing at its heels.

I got up to use the bathroom, and groped around for something to keep me warm. Seeing Stella nestled snugly under the comforter, I curbed a mean-spirited impulse to snag it, and fetched my trench coat. It would do as a makeshift blanket.

Eventually, I sank into a restless slumber, uncaring whether my *alleged* snoring, something Stella held over my head, filled the room.

CHAPTER FIVE

I awoke to an empty apartment. No welcoming aroma of freshly brewing coffee. No hint of Stella's perfume. No hiss of bacon and eggs frying in the pan.

It was awful.

Instead, I was greeted by a note propped on the end table. I knew the author, of course, but the hurried scrawl told me, in no uncertain terms, that she was still furious.

> *Butterfield,*
>
> *I suggest you keep your promise regarding your latest conquest. I am going to the office to arrange a meeting with Mr. Russo.*

There were no endearments, none of the usual humorous undertones I have come to expect from my partner. Just a frosty directive, as though I was nothing more than an employee.

Her continued allusion to a supposed affair gnawed at

me. I had no idea what to say to convince her that Mrs. Peterson, however rich and… available… left me cold.

Frustrated, I crumpled the note and tossed it into the trash as I crossed to the phone. Lifting the heavy black receiver from the cradle, I dialed Walnut-9565, a number I had committed to memory.

The phone rang twice before a man with a pinched nasally voice answered, "Peterson residence. How may I help you?"

I recognized the voice as belonging to Jamison, the Petersons' butler. Much to his chagrin, it had become my habit — inspired by one of my favorite books — to greet him by a different but, to my way of thinking, far more fitting name.

"Jeeves, it's Butterfield…" A prolonged and discouraging groan echoed through the phone — his standard reaction. "…is the lady of the house home?"

"Mrs. Peterson is not available at the moment. Is there a message you wish me to convey?"

I hesitated, unsure whether to trust Jamison to pass on anything I had to say, preferring to speak to my client directly, to avoid the risk of confusion.

"Never mind, Jeeves, I'll try again later.

"As you wish." The line went dead before I had the chance to respond. I replaced the handset, staring at the phone absently while a whole other scene played out in my head.

What was Stella doing?

Neither of us had unblemished pasts. Half the reason we were together was precisely because the waters around us were murky, but I had never given her any cause to doubt my commitment to her and our business partnership.

She had to realize I was no cheat.

My father was unfaithful to my mother, too many times to count, and I saw the harm it did to her, never mind how many adultery cases we had taken. The trail of damage was irreparable and damning.

I vowed long ago, never to inflict that on anyone, especially Stella. Somewhere along the way, she had become an integral part of my life, even if neither of us would ever contemplate saying *I do...* officially.

Stella's sudden cynicism, and the gradual yet undeniable distance yawning between us, perturbed me, but I could not think how to close the gap, or restore our relationship.

Washed and dressed, I coerced my sleep-deprived body to Clara's for a quick bite to eat and the, hopefully, reviving cup or three of hot coffee. Clara greeted me with her usual cheerful banter.

If Stella had been here earlier to gripe about me, Clara did not betray her trust. The grizzled woman gave no hint either way, which I appreciated. Small miracles.

The way I felt this morning, I could not possibly handle a cold shoulder from Clara on top of everything else.

Yes, I was feeling sorry for myself... so sue me.

Stomach full, and the coffee doing its therapeutic pirouette along my synapses, I tipped my hat to the diner's namesake, walked out into the sunshine, and drove to the office.

Stella was there, perched on her desk, talking to someone on the phone. From her dulcet tones, I guessed it to be God's gift to lowly private eyes — Mr. Carmine Russo.

"Just toot when you get here and I'll meet you downstairs," she trilled brightly.

I suppressed the grimace I felt forming and waited.

Stella knew I was there but took out her compact to inspect her makeup and hair. Apparently happy with her reflection, she plucked her jacket off the hat stand, and slipped it on. Only then did she face me.

This was part of her game, her way of teaching me whatever lesson she believed I needed to learn, but I was not in the mood and refused to give her the satisfaction of letting her goad me.

"Oh, Jacob, there you are. I hope you slept well," she cooed insincerely. "I have to go out. Did you speak to Mrs. Peterson?" She could not help a derisive curl of her lip when she said *our* client's name.

"She was unavailable. Don't worry," I said before Stella could interject with another snooty remark. "I'll keep trying."

"See you do."

"Stella, I have no clue what's caused this…" I waved my hand between us awkwardly. I could talk the birds out of the sky when it came to clients, criminals, and cops… generally… but heart-to-heart conversations were not my forte. "What have I done? What happened?" I knew I sounded plaintive, bordering on outright whining, but I was at a complete loss.

Stella studied me for so long, I could picture the cogs grinding in her brain. Her gaze dropped, dark lashes sweeping over the smooth curve of her cheeks, flawlessly applied make up covering the sprinkling of freckles she hated. Then her eyes rose to meet mine, and I read, not the anger I braced myself for, but resignation.

"Do you really need me to spell it out?"

"Frankly, yes."

"I'm sorry, I have neither the time nor the energy right now. You are not a child, Jacob, think it through. Apply the same effort to the problem as you afford our clients. I have to go."

A horn blew somewhere below us… the speed with which Russo arrived indicated he must have called her from around the corner. That the sleaze was so certain she would drop everything to join him, intensified my resentment.

"That's my ride." Stella slung her purse over her shoulder and picked up a file. "I'll see you later."

"You don't want me to come?" I heard the desperation in my voice and cursed myself. *Get a grip, Butters.*

"Not today." She blew me a kiss as she walked out.

Perhaps there was some hope for us.

"Take care," I called after her, hearing an "always," float back to me as the door swung closed.

I sat at my desk and scowled at the pile of papers in front of me.

Those three coffees were not nearly enough.

CHAPTER SIX

The day dragged with mind-numbing slowness. I completed as much of the paperwork as I could, but most were at the invoicing stage, and Stella refused to let me near the billing side of things. I made do with clipping notes to anything requiring her attention.

By mid-afternoon, I was twiddling my thumbs.

I had tried the Peterson residence several times and was beginning to question whether Jamison had a sixth sense because the phone rang out every time. I was determined not to schlep over there and give Stella another excuse to accuse me of something I hadn't done.

Eventually, I went home, hoping my dearly beloved partner might be there, but the apartment was cold and quiet. Not even the screech of Mrs. Harper's radio penetrated the silence... a first.

I opened a beer and stood at the window watching the world go by below me; my mind, a chaotic battleground one minute and desolate void the next. No matter how I tried to wrest my thoughts into some form of coherence they skittered off on a tangent.

I hated feeling adrift.

Stella was the one person who believed in me, who encouraged me to take this leap of faith and become a private detective. I thought we were good together. Images chased through my mind like one of those moving pictures at the Roxie.

I sank onto the couch and did what I had been putting off all day.

An hour later and no closer to figuring out my supposed transgressions, I heaved myself upright to ring Mrs. Peterson for the umpteenth time.

Finally, Jamison answered. I was hard pushed not to be snippy but strove for courtesy. I needed him on my side.

"Jeeves, my good man. Is Mrs. Peterson available to speak with me now?" I infused a cheerful note into my question.

I heard a quickly muted sniff, followed by, "Mrs. Peterson is about to leave for dinner with friends, sir."

"I won't keep her from her engagement, but this is important. Please." Maybe because I rarely used pleasantries when talking to the butler, my entreaty seemed to do the trick.

There was silence on the other end of the line as, doubtless, Jamison debated with himself as to whether it was better to interrupt his mistress now or suffer me calling *ad nauseam* until I got my way.

I knew he had opted for the former when I heard his aggrieved harrumph. "Very well, sir, but I cannot promise."

I heard a soft clink as Jamison put the handset down, followed by the clip of his footsteps on the marble-tiled floor of the entrance hall as he walked away.

Shortly thereafter, the slightly out-of-breath, perky tones of Eleanor Peterson filled the receiver. "Jake, darling, I was just thinking about you. To what do I owe this joyful call?"

"Mrs. Peterson—" I started, to be waylaid by my client's determination to dispense with formalities.

"Jake, how many times must I reiterate? It's Eleanor or preferably, Ellie… to you." Her voice dropped to what Stella would describe as a seductive murmur, and I heard my partner's, "I told you so," reverberating around my skull.

This was a conversation best served without hostilities, so I laid on the charm. "Ellie, I have some news you'll want to hear in person. Can you meet me tomorrow morning at Clara's Diner? It's closer to you than my office."

"U-uh, why not meet *at* your office?" Ellie proposed coyly.

The image of Stella stewing at her desk when Eleanor walked in put the kibosh on that idea.

Before I replied, she all but purred, "Better still, come here. Paul is away this week, as usual, and I could send Jamison on a few errands while we two spend some quality time together discussing whatever trivial matter you—"

It was then I realized Jamison was lying to me about Eleanor being on her way out for a dinner date.

Go figure.

"No, Mrs… Ellie, that's not possible. We must meet tomorrow morning, and at Clara's," my tone, adamant.

For a long moment, the line went quiet, then she said, "I don't know what this is all about, dear, but I'll be there around ten."

The sharp click of the receiver cut the call, leaving me to stare at the phone, wondering how we had gone from Mr. Butterfield and Mrs. Peterson to Jake and Ellie… and, worse, darling and dear.

It was well after midnight when Stella came home. Gallant as ever, I had taken the couch with a suitable blanket this time, so as not to cause a scene, and pretended to be asleep when she crept in.

The scent of Cuban cigars, perfume, and a hint of spirits followed her, filling my nostrils as she read the note I had left, outlining my conversation with Mrs. Peterson.

It was another long and uncomfortable night. When I woke around eight, Stella and the note were gone. If I was being fanciful, I might say her absence was a reflection on the state of our union… as it were, although I tried not to place too much significance on it.

I knew why Stella had no qualms about where I was meeting Mrs. Peterson, evidenced by her lack of reply to my note. Clara has ears like a bat and would flit around like a mother hen, eavesdropping on any information she imagined Stella might find useful.

Her network of spies was almost *as comprehensive as Gil's.*

At the chime of the bell, Clara, in place of her usual friendly greeting, nodded and pointed to a booth in the far corner of the cafe. Presumably, Stella had told her I was coming.

I noticed the clock on the wall behind the counter read five past ten. Was Eleanor already here? I scanned the diner, relieved to see I was first to arrive.

Taking a seat, I watched Clara bring two mugs and a pot of coffee. No menus, she just filled the cups, then glanced at the front door.

"I believe I see your guest, Mr. Butterfield. Miss Fitzhugh gave me a good description."

Stella had met Mrs Peterson once, the day she requested

our services, and I was taken aback by Clara's remark, although why, eluded me. My partner possessed an uncanny knack for committing even the most insignificant details to memory. The fact, she recalled *our* client's appearance ought not to be a surprise but this morning it was. Two sleepless nights will do that.

I dragged my attention back to Clara who left the pot on the table, with a piece of advice, "Hurry up and get this done, Jacob, then clear out. Your girl won't wait forever."

With that, Clara returned to her spot behind the counter… easily within earshot.

The door swung open to reveal Eleanor Peterson. Smiling radiantly, she hurried to join me in the booth, shed her coat, sat down, and inched close, looping her arm through mine.

Clara's brows lowered.

"Now, what has you in such a lather, you had to see me so urgently and at a time the birds refuse to acknowledge?"

Ignoring the fact most people had been up for hours, I skittered away from her like a cat on a hot tin roof, casting a wary glance at Clara and then back to Ellie.

"Mrs. Peters… Ellie, this is your file," I indicated the buff folder on the table between us, "in which there is more than enough evidence against your husband to ensure you will want for nothing for the rest of your life."

"You, mean we?" Eleanor gazed at me with doe eyes.

"Excuse me?" I asked, with what had to be a dumbfounded look on my face.

"*We* will want for nothing. You and I, Jake. We will be free to go anywhere in the world. Do anything, we want. That was always the plan, yes?"

"N-*No*," I expostulated. "There was never anything except catching your husband with his secretary."

Eleanor blanched, her smile crumpled and her face

contorted into something resembling a death mask. "H-how can you say that, Jacob? After all the time we spent together. Surely, you felt the attraction, too. It wasn't just my imagination."

"Mrs. Peterson—"

"*Mrs. Peterson?*" Eleanor squawked. "Is that all I am to you? Just a client?"

This was not going well at all. "I have no doubt you are a wonderful person," I hedged diplomatically, "but you must understand, you hired me to do a job…"

My effort to be honest yet empathetic, along with the rest of my impromptu exculpation, fell on deaf ears. Rising to her feet, Eleanor vented her spleen in the form of a solid slap across my cheek. An explosion of stars performed a dizzying jig in front of my eyes.

I'm sure I heard Clara snickering over the bells jangling in my ears.

Trying to rescue the rapidly deteriorating situation, I offered her the paperwork, willing her to take it to end this debacle once and for all.

Ranting about ingrates, and pathetic losers, and men being the root of all evil… this last, to be fair, I could not deny, Eleanor grabbed the file and proceeded to beat me about the head with it, and boy, she did not hold back.

Palms up to deflect her attack, I tried to placate the enraged woman… a waste of breath… and before I could get a word in edgeways was doused in a blizzard of dollar bills.

"If this isn't enough to buy your love, Jacob Butterfield, then to hell with you."

My head smarting, and money slithering off me to decorate the booth, I watched Eleanor Peterson storm out of the diner. Clara, no longer trying to restrain her amusement, chortled with laughter.

Embarrassed, an emotion foreign to yours truly, and speechless, I picked up Eleanor's final payment, laid one of the dollar bills on the table to cover the coffee, and left with what was left of my dignity.

CHAPTER SEVEN

I did not anticipate the meeting with Eleanor Peterson to end so abruptly... or badly. Shrugging it off, a quick glance at my watch confirmed the whole thing had played out in under twenty minutes.

Outside the diner, I pondered my options, then decided to drive to the office on the off-chance Stella was there.

No such luck *but*, there was a scribbled, if terse, message. A time and an address. The latter sounded familiar, and, opening a drawer, I retrieved our Rand McNally city map, jabbing my finger on the well-used paper when my hunch proved correct.

Quashing my irritation at the growing feeling I was being manipulated, I hopped back into the DeSoto and wound my way through the busy mid-morning traffic.

While I really wanted this Russo character to be holed up at a local Y, in bunk number thirteen, underneath a hole in the roof, I doubted the neighborhood I was approaching would ever approve such an institution, or that Russo was a resident. It was a convenient place to meet — discretion guaranteed.

Entering the Nob Hill District of the City by the Bay, the change in prestige at this side of town was pronounced. It boasted, *look at my bank account.*

Negotiating the leafy, winding streets, I cruised to a halt in front of the King's Swan Inn, parked, and viewed the façade. Like every other similarly managed establishment, a kid with a greasy haircut met me at my car door.

He opened it and, as I climbed out, upturned his palm for the keys, his greeting as slick as the top of his head. "Welcome to the King's Swan Inn, sir. The finest inn and restaurant in the city."

These places rarely matched the hype but dissuading him of what I suspected to be blatant exaggeration to attract the *It* crowd was pointless, so I made do with nodding an acknowledgement.

"You have an exquisite vehicle, sir. Dare I say a classic? It'll be safe with me, sir."

The more the kid slathered on the compliments, the bigger the tip I was supposed to pay. I got him in my car and away from the front door with a five-dollar tip. It was a good thing my immediate past included being pelted by an angry handful of cash.

I entered the restaurant but did not inform the maître d' I was waiting for anyone else. Taking the proffered seat, I ordered a club sandwich and two fingers of bourbon.

My seat angled so as not to miss any arrivals, I ate my meal as slowly as possible.

About forty-five minutes and three more bourbons later, I saw Stella enter, preceding a large man who held the door open for her, with old-world courtesy. I swore she preened a little at the chivalrous gesture, which did not improve my mood one jot.

The cut of the gorilla's suit along with his oily appearance marked him as a gangster. A fact to which Stella was either oblivious, or had chosen to ignore, because his crooked grin confirmed my suspicions.

My enchanting partner had accepted the case, and the goon was elated she had.

My stomach rebelled… *and, no, it had nothing to do with the bourbons and club sandwich.*

Stella's expression was unreadable when she met my eyes across the room, leaving me perplexed and uneasy.

Was she happy I had beaten them to the venue, meaning I had fulfilled our contract with Eleanor Peterson, or disappointed not to be able to spend more time alone with the lug? It would remain a mystery.

I rose as she approached, something Mother Butterfield had instilled in all her children at the business end of a wooden serving spoon.

Instead of brushing my cheek with her habitual kiss, she made herself comfortable on an adjacent chair and waited for Russo to join us.

"Mister Butterfield, I presume," her companion drawled. "Carmine Russo." He extended his bulky hand, which I shook with a show of affability, then sank his bulk into the remaining seat, and clicked his fat fingers.

A waiter materialized at Russo's elbow ready to take drink orders. Already buzzing after my quartet of bourbons and determined not to miss a single word of the ensuing conversation, I opted for a coffee.

Russo, on the other hand, had no such reservations. "I'll have a whiskey highball…" he gave Stella a conspiratorial wink, as though they shared a joke, "…and the little lady here will have a *dirty* martini."

Little lady? I wanted to gag… stunned when the little lady blushed demurely.

Once the drinks were served and we were as alone as anyone can be in a popular restaurant, I broached the business at hand, "Mister Russo… Carmine," I amended at the tilt of his head, "my partner has acquainted me with the particulars of the theft, but before we sign on the dotted line, so to speak…"

Russo sent Stella a curious look, one I interpreted as meaning that, without my knowledge or agreement, the contract was already approved. At her lack of response, he returned his attention to me, as I corralled my thoughts.

"…I have one or two… details, which require…" I scoured my brain for a suitable term, coming up with, "fine tuning."

"I expected nothing less." Russo smiled but it was directed at Stella, whose lips twitched. A sliver of animosity flickered through me, and I felt the sting of Stella's disloyalty, aware I had been the subject of discussion between them.

"Why our agency?"

"You are small and discreet. I've heard good things." Russo replied, smoothly.

From Stella, no doubt, I ground my teeth inwardly.

Fingers steepled under my chin, I studied him speculatively. "Interesting, although I am unsure what *good things* you would hear about a firm run by a discredited former homicide detective." Gratified to see him wince when his own, less than polite, observation was thrown back at him, and leaving him in no doubt as to Stella's exhaustive report of their first meeting.

Treating me to a death stare, Stella pressed her shoe on mine, hard. I shot her a stony look in return, annoyed that Russo was witnessing this peculiar and, to my mind, inexplicable fracturing of our partnership.

Nevertheless, mine was the name on the door and,

despite my conviction that Stella had taken the case, heedless of my opinion, she was not running the show… yet. I turned my attention to the man who, at least, had the grace to flush.

"Mister Butterfield, I do not want to get off on the wrong foot."

He smiled… at me this time. "I have contacts, many, *many* contacts who do their due diligence when it comes to anything requiring a high degree of confidentiality. I do not trust just anyone… ever. So, yes, I know your history, but that is precisely why I chose you," he included Stella in his answer. "You have more to lose than a gumshoe with an impeccable background, so you will not cut corners or try to scam me. Never mind that, should you be tempted, you will…"

"…end up swimming with the fishes," I interrupted caustically.

"I did not say that." Russo countered mildly.

"Maybe, but that, I think, would apply to whomever you contacted, irrespective of their… integrity." I posited rhetorically. "Yeah. Yeah." I flapped my hand at Stella whose thunderous countenance did not bode well for an entente any time soon.

I swallowed my aggravation. There were three factors for consideration. One, Stella wanted us to take the case, and I had no wish to be stuck in her bad books because I turned it down. Two, I could not deny we needed the money. Three and, in all honesty, the deciding factor — Russo being a member of the mob… I am not an idiot… aside — it sounded intriguing. I can never ignore intriguing.

"Let's get down to brass tacks, shall we?" I said in tacit, albeit belated, confirmation we had accepted the job. "Can you describe the layout of the room where the safe was located, better still, how about we drive out to the place to see it first-hand."

"That won't be necessary, Jacob," Stella said. "Mister Russo took me to the estate yesterday." She pulled a stencil pad from her purse and passed it to me.

That explained the phone call. I flipped through the pages. Stella had done an excellent job of impersonating an architect with her meticulous sketches of what appeared to be every room in the house.

I glanced at my partner, who was discussing possible exit points from the estate with Russo.

She had also drawn the safe, which I recognized, from my days in the SFPD, as a Gruenwald 6000. Someone had paid a pretty penny for this baby, and the person who had broken into it, was either a professional, had the combination, or forced whoever did.

"Looks like your boss spent a fortune on his safe," I interrupted their conversation.

"Yeah," Russo acknowledged. "Nothing but the best will do."

"If that's the case, how do you explain someone waltzing into his house and cracking a supposedly unbreakable safe, so easily?"

"Obviously," Russo grumbled irritably, "it was done by a pro."

"But who would be familiar with the contents?" I pressed.

"How the hell am I supposed to know?" Russo shot back.

I guess that struck a nerve. I tried to soften my manner and nodded to him in outward understanding.

He must have assumed this to be condescension or feigned because the crimson stain warming his cheeks was undeniable.

"Maybe one of the maids saw what was in there? They skulk about the estate like Ali Baba's forty thieves. If you're insinuating anything else, I can—"

Whatever else he was going to say was lost because Stella,

in overt indication she was reaching the end of her tether at what she considered to be my ignorant behaviour, rammed her stiletto heel into the toe of my polished shoe.

"Ouch, dammit." Aware of our salubrious surroundings, I smothered an agonized yell with difficulty, and we glowered at each other like cats circling for a fight.

Stella broke eye contact first, heaving a long-suffering sigh. "Mister Russo, please forgive Mister Butterfield's rudeness. I'm afraid his years as a cop have tainted his opinion of mankind."

Russo chuckled at Stella's observation. "Don't fret, doll. I'm used to dealing with guys like him."

He addressed me again, but his attitude had changed, "I'll tell ya what, Butterfield, feel free to talk to any of the help, although Miss Fitzhugh here has beaten you to most of them and unearthed nothing of value. If that's what it takes, I've no objection. My only proviso is that you're not allowed to set foot on the estate."

"How am I supposed to investigate anything if I'm hamstrung by your ridiculous conditions?" I contested sourly.

"Quite simple, Butters," Stella intervened sedately. "You tell me what you want to know, and I'll pass it onto Carmine."

"*Carmine?*" I repeated, remembering her very recent and full-fledged meltdown about Eleanor Peterson.

Stella refused to bite.

Russo clarified, "Miss Fitzhugh is the best conduit between us. I have come to neither like nor trust you, sir."

"The feeling is mutual, Russo," I muttered darkly.

Employing her best schoolmarm tone, Stella separated the fighting children. "Boys, enough. Carmine, perhaps it's time we concluded negotiations. Could you take me home?"

"Sure, doll."

Rising to leave with the gangster, Stella issued me with an order, "Jacob, you should track down Gil to see whether he's learned anything."

With that, I was alone at the table, just in time to have the waiter present me with the check for the meeting.

I scotched the compulsion flip off my luncheon guests in absentia, conceding there was no point if they were not present to revel in its glory.

CHAPTER EIGHT

When I left the inn, it was coming up to half past two. Being a Thursday, I knew my friend would be getting his hair cut.

Creature of habit. I grinned to myself.

Driving through The Embarcadero, I headed to the only place I knew Detective Frank Gilbert trusted to touch his precious hair, Randazzo's Barber Shop.

My, wholly unnecessary, glance through the window to confirm my supposition was rewarded when, sure enough, there in the third of the four barber's chairs, sat the paragon of rectitude, the eminent police sergeant.

He appeared to be embroiled in a spirited debate with the proprietor, Julius Randazzo, while the older man clipped. To assign this task to an underling would be sacrilege.

Entering the shop, I was hit with the scent of bay rum and pomade, as both men stopped speaking to look at the door. Randazzo pointed with his comb to an empty chair to wait my turn, then returned to the subject under discussion.

"I am telling you," Randazzo pressed with the intensity of a congressman trying to get his legislation passed. "If

Roosevelt doesn't stop sitting on his hands, Hitler and his troops will be knocking on the door of the White House, demanding the keys to the place."

"Calm down, Julius. You know stress is bad for your heart."

"Bah," the barber grumbled. "It won't matter when the Third Reich is marching down Pennsylvania Avenue. Just look what happened in Paris."

"Okay, okay, I'll make sure to write to my representative, urging him to vote to bomb Berlin immediately."

"Joke all you want, Frank. People did the same thing in sixteen when Wilson was in office, and the next thing you knew, the Germans were sinking our ships and planning to invade Texas through Mexico. But why should you understand? You were no doubt in knee pants at the time."

Spying the barber's puce cheeks, I decided a tactful intervention was prudent. "How about you change topics before Julius slits your throat? What about football? Gil, you're a big Green Bay fan, what do—"

"Christ, Butterfield, are you trying to get me stabbed?"

"Huh?" I gaped at him in confusion.

"Don't you know Randazzo here is a diehard Bears fan, and they play each other Sunday?"

Randazzo jabbed Gil with his scissors, *accidently*, before resuming the haircut. "Don't forget you'll owe me ten dollars when we beat you."

"In your dreams, old man," Gil ribbed, then eyed me balefully. "How about you stop causing me to lose blood, Butterfield, and tell me why you're here, as if I didn't know."

I inclined my head towards Randazzo, trying to inquire, without words, whether it was safe to have this conversation in the barber's presence.

Gil chuckled. "Butterfield, you know barbershops are as notorious for gossip as any beauty salon. Hell, ol' Julius here is my best source of information, and he knows he can't spill anything to anyone else besides me, otherwise he'll lose my business. He sure as hell doesn't want that, because the entire San Francisco police department will go with me."

Gil was not one for idle threats, and I knew Julius had been the force's barbershop of choice for more years than I cared to count.

Years later, long after Julius Randazzo's death, I learned he had served in the First World War as an Austro-Hungarian code breaker for Great Britain's Secret Service Bureau, now known as MI6. Gathering, judging the value of, and disseminating secrets came naturally to him.

After emigrating to America, he had set up shop in Chicago, where he continued to hone his eavesdropping skills by providing invaluable information about the activities of certain mafia families for that fine city's Police Department.

Eventually, the bitter Chicago winters became unbearable, and he moved west to the warmer climes of California, settling in San Francisco.

One of his first customers was Frank Gilbert and, whoa, did the barber have a story to share with him.

Julius flashed a smile at me, while he worked on Gil's million-dollar haircut, then all animation drained from his face as he, presumably, disconnected from our conversation.

A valuable skill, and one I wish I had mastered long ago.

"Okay, fine," I relented. "What do your people know about the diamond heist?"

"That's the funny thing. As famous as that stone is…was… however you want to describe it, there's not a peep about it on the streets. No one is trying to fence it or cut it. My guy in the jewelry district said, the only thing he heard is that if the rumors of who actually owns the bauble are correct, you need to tread on eggshells, Jake."

"I figured that much out on my own, Gil. I've met the guy's stuffed suit."

"I'm serious, bud. We are talking East Coast muscle and money."

"I appreciate your concern, mom, but I'll be okay."

"See you are. I really don't want my next haircut to be for your funeral."

"I'm sure Randazzo there could give you a fancy widow's peak, if need be," I joked, but did not manage to get so much as a flicker of a grin from Gil, though I could have sworn Julius's scissors stilled for just a second.

Gil blew out his cheeks. "I'm sure you've been out to the estate to take a look—"

"No, no I haven't, and it doesn't look like that's likely anytime soon or at all."

"How are you supposed to find the perp?" Gil frowned in puzzlement.

"That's a question you're gonna have to ask your cousin. Stella is the only one allowed on the premises. I can't even interview the help on site. Her self-appointed *escort...*" my lip curled, "...is being deliberately obstructive."

"Bowled him over him with your winning personality did ya, Butters?"

I glared at Frank, and my retort slipped out, "Can it, Gil. I'm getting enough grief from my partner without hearing it from you, as well."

"Christ, Jacob. No need to get all hot under the collar."

My friend's shock registered, and I drew a calming breath. "I'm sorry, Gil. I shouldn't have snapped at you like that. Things aren't good between Stella and me right now."

"Yeah, my wife told me."

"Wow, I didn't realize it had reached the point that Stella needed to involve family."

"All's I'll say is that I wouldn't let it fester much longer.

Anyway, back to your conundrum. I might be able to help you with background on the staff."

"I'd appreciate it, because I have no idea how anyone could waltz into a place like that, break into a safe, and get away without being seen, unless it was an inside job."

"Can't help with the hatchet men who hang out there but, as for staff, most of the moneyed types go through the same employment agency. It's run by a woman named Millicent Wallace." He gave me the address, which I wrote down under her name in my handy-dandy notebook.

Stuffing it into my coat pocket, I rose to leave.

Gil farewelled me with a piece of advice, "I know you, Butterfield. Be a gentleman."

"Meaning?"

"You'll understand when you see her."

Not getting anything else from Frank Gilbert, I nodded at the two men. It was only then that Julius responded.

Climbing into my DeSoto, I glanced in the rearview mirror as I drew away from the curb to see a silver and gray, late model La Salle Series 50 pull out of a parking spot, three cars behind me.

The two goons in the front seat looked out of place in this section of town, so I took a short detour to make me feel less paranoid. After the third turn, it was obvious they were following me. Now I had to figure out who sent them.

Cruising to a halt in front of the sturdy brick building which housed the Wallace Employment Agency, I stayed in my car until I saw the La Salle slide into a space further down the street.

The driver was in dire need of a lesson, or six, in how to tail someone covertly.

Alighting, I stared at the car for a long moment, then shook my head, uncaring whether they saw my derisive disbelief.

A smartly dressed, bottle-blonde woman... *was that the hair color every woman in California wanted to sport...* seated behind an antique desk, stood in practiced greeting.

"Good afternoon, sir." She scanned an open appointment book. "Do you have a meeting scheduled with Madame Wallace? She is a busy woman."

Flashing my badge, I replied, "No, but I do need to speak with her. A matter of utmost importance pertaining to the reputation of her company."

Apparently unmoved by my credentials and mission, the receptionist stared at me for a long moment, then lifted the handset of the phone on her desk, and pressed a button. "I apologise for the interruption, ma'am, but there is a man here making wild claims about a threat to your company. Should I send him on his way?"

After a brief silence, she said, "Yes, ma'am, I will."

Replacing the receiver on its cradle, she regarded me sternly, and pointed to a chair against a far wall. "Madame Wallace will be with you shortly."

Apparently, 'shortly' was a relative concept as minutes became an hour... or so my watch told me. I sent the receptionist several dirty looks, indicating the clock was ticking. She shrugged indifferently, then ignored me altogether.

Fed up, I was about to make a scene, when a pinched voice reached my ears from somewhere behind me.

"Mister Butterfield, forgive my tardiness." A short, stout woman, appeared from a dim corridor. "Please join me in my office, where I will be happy to answer your questions to the best of my ability."

Her knowledge of my name and purpose meant, while I was cooling my heels, the woman had spoken to someone about me.

The office was well-appointed, and decorated in the — if I recalled the magazines Stella read avidly, correctly — streamlined and modernist Art Deco style. With a nod, Madam Wallace directed me to a chair adjacent to an elegant rosewood table.

After we had taken our respective seats, the proprietress assessed me briefly and in silence. A tactic, I suspected, she employed on prospective hires, and which, save one wholly ungentlemanly reaction, had no effect on me.

Dispassionately, I held her gaze… or tried to. Face to face with Madam Wallace, I understood Gil's warning. The woman's eyes wandered around her sockets, seemingly independent of each other, reminding me of a certain fish I had caught on a trip up north years ago.

With Stella's repeated and aggrieved warnings about offending people, especially anyone with a recognized medical condition, ringing in my head, I made a concerted effort *not* to address her as Miss Walleye.

"How may I be of help?" her tone was polite, verging on amenable.

I nipped the skin on my wrist… hard, which had the desired result. Schooling my features, I said with no hint of sarcasm, "I am sorry for interrupting your busy day but, during the course of my enquiries into a… sensitive case, it has become imperative to question you about the staff you assigned to the estate—"

"Yes, I was informed as much."

She crossed to a bank of filing cabinets, extracted a single folder from the middle one, and handed it to me. "I believe everything you need is in here."

"Um, excuse me, Madam Walle...Wallace," I caught myself, preventing an egregious faux pas. "I have specific questions for you."

"I'm afraid I do not have time to discuss my staff with you any further, Mister Butterfield. Please show yourself out."

Her curt dismissal brooked no argument. I considered pressing my point but, one look at her rigid demeanor, informed me it was a waste of breath. I rose, tucked the folder under my arm, and tipped my hat at the woman, who treated my courtesy with glacial indifference.

Wow!

Back in my car, I thumbed through the folder, which contained a list of employees hired for the estate, as well as a criminal and financial background on each.

Every record appeared to be clean. Not even so much as a traffic ticket. While none of those hired were wealthy by any stretch of the imagination, each appeared to be comfortable.

Engrossed in the files, it took several seconds to register a gentle tapping on my window. Sadly, it was not a raven trying to attract my attention, but the business end of an ugly .38 revolver, wielded by an even uglier thug.

His clone stood at the passenger side, pistol drawn, presumably on the off-chance I decided to dive out of that door.

Looking at the *gentleman* on my side, I saw him motion with his popgun to wind down the window. Summoning up a pleasant smile, I said, "Whatever you two Girl Scouts are selling, I'm afraid I don't have the money today."

"Hand over your pieces, Butterfield, both of them."

"Piece? Piece of what? I have a piece of gum," I patted my pockets, "but you're gonna have to share it with your friend there."

Not amused by my banter, he leaned in to rest the barrel of his .38 on the bridge of my nose. "You're a comedian, Butterfield. It's a good thing the boss wants to speak with you, or I'd plug ya now and be done with you."

Extracting my pistol from its holster, and the one strapped to my ankle, I did as instructed.

Dropping them into his pocket, he opened my door, and nodded down the street, "I'm sure you know which car to get into."

CHAPTER NINE

We pulled up in front of a mansion which complemented the La Salle… opulent and obsolete.

In the same way that the vehicle I had been *ushered* into, a gun jammed in my ribs, was no longer produced by Cadillac, under the auspices of belonging to another time… so, the architecture of the house evoked the antiquated era of Queen Victoria, paid for with San Francisco gold, which had long since dried up.

Propelled under the front portico, *a word I had always wanted to use*, and through a set of front doors designed to impress invited guests and deter everyone else, I was escorted across the atrium then along a hall to a small office.

Seated in an armchair, smoking a cigarette and talking on the phone, a well-groomed man whom I recognized from his pictures in the newspapers… and his wanted poster.

Mr. Dino Antonnelli.

Before I could speak, he held up one finger to silence me. Not something I take kindly to but I curbed my tongue.

"Yeah, he's here right now. No, I don't know why it took him so long to show up, I guess he was waiting for some official summons. Russo? Last I saw he was chasing some floozy in a skirt…"

His derogatory description of my partner rankled. Bad enough that, after *requesting* my presence, this bozo was ignoring me, but denigrating Stella, who I presumed was in essence a stranger to him, did nothing to mitigate my contempt.

"Honestly, I don't know why you bother with that lug. He's a schmuck. We have better qualified people… yeah, yeah… he's your boy. Just remember that when all hell breaks loose."

He hung up the phone, then, without so much as a nod, never mind a good afternoon, unleashed a brutal right hook, nearly knocking me out of the chair.

"You heard what I told my friend, bud. Do you think my boss will pay you for sitting on your ass?"

"And hello to you as well, Mr. Antonelli."

"So, you know who I am?"

"Who can't pick up a paper and not see your mug splattered all over it?" I scoffed, rubbing my jaw.

Dino "Dice" Antonelli — *why gangsters insist on having nicknames that sound like characters from Dick Tracy, I can never figure out* — bunched his fist.

Fed up with the whole scenario, and quite prepared to flatten this knucklehead, I leapt to my feet in a defensive stance.

"I'm glad to see you're not as much of a pushover as I was beginning to think." He chuckled. "Now, answer my question, Butterfield. Why haven't I seen you around the estate? How do you expect to find the diamond if you don't bother to investigate the scene of the crime?

"That dame Russo had out here was easy on the eyes, mind," Antonelli mused, making me wonder whether he was oblivious to Stella being more than just my business partner, "but women like that are only good for one thing, and it ain't being a dick. More like enjoying one."

He laughed at his own joke. At least he found himself hilarious.

Silently, I counted to ten in an effort to control the temptation to punch him into the middle of next year.

"Miss Fitzhugh is a throughly capable investigator—" I championed Stella, to be cut off with...

"Maybe, but she ain't you, and that's who we wanted for this job."

"In that case, instead of beating me to death, perhaps it might be an idea to show me around, while you explain why Russo didn't want me here."

On my guard, I watched as, resuming his seat, Antonelli assessed me. Presumably, whatever he saw was satisfactory because he said, "Fine, I suppose you ought to see it, though it'd be fun to go a few more rounds with you first. I could do with a sparring partner and you make a good punching bag."

"Generous offer, but no thanks." I declined glibly.

"Sure?" Antonelli arched a brow, amusement lurking in his sharp eyes.

With the merest hint of a grin, I nodded, drawing an acknowledgement in kind from my host, and the tension between us subsided.

"Another time perhaps. As for Russo, I presume he prefers to keep you at a distance so he can have his way with your girl..." which cleared up my misconceptions of just how much Antonelli knew about me... "that's how he operates. Anyway, I have more important things to do than worry about your love life, Butterfield, let me show you the safe and we can go from there."

Antonelli led the way down a wood and mirror paneled corridor to a set of oak double doors. I waited as he tugged on a hefty key ring, secured to his belt by a chain, reminiscent of a school janitor.

In any other situation, the length of time it took him to find the requisite key, which he slid into the lock, would be comical, but now was probably *not* the best time to give into mirth.

A loud click, and the door opened onto a sizable office. Before entering, I knelt to examine the locking mechanism.

"Tell me, Mr. Antonelli, or would you rather I call you Dice?" I asked, a trace of sarcasm in my tone.

"You can call me whatever you like as long as you solve this case," came the brusque reply.

"Is this door always locked?"

"Of course. People don't just wander around here like it's a museum with public access."

"Then can you explain the lack of pick marks on the lock? I mean, yeah, I can see where the key has taken its toll on the keyhole, but... and I'm sure in *your* business you have come upon a sprung lock or two... none of that is obvious here."

Antonelli grimaced at the realization no one had bothered to check such a simple detail.

Gratified that I had already found an easily overlooked clue, especially in front of this ass, I brushed past him into a room, which was elaborate to the point of gauche — and this was just the office.

Hoping to catch my host off guard, I asked over my shoulder while scanning the space, "Given that jangling mess on your belt, I take it you're the number two guy in this racket?"

He took the question in his stride. "Hardly, who would want that headache. I'm more a... peacemaker... if you will." The pride in his voice was unmistakable.

"The outfit's consigliere, in fact."

"Mr. Butterfield." Antonelli gave a wry chuckle. "I'm afraid you spend too much time watching gangster movies at the Orpheum. I'm just the in-house lawyer guarding my employer's business interests.

"Yeah, Murder Incorporated," I muttered, making a beeline to the expensive safe.

"What was that?" Antonelli quizzed as he joined me.

"I asked whether anything has been moved."

"No, not since the robbery."

Inspecting the massive dial on the safe, I noticed, like the door's lock, there were no marks. Whoever stole the diamond had unrestricted access to this room and the safe.

"Besides you and my mysterious employer, who else uses this room?"

"No one, without an escort."

"Are you confessing, Dice?" a voice boomed behind us.

In unison, we turned to see Carmine Russo propped against the door jamb. Our attention gained, he straightened up and nodded at me, "What's that rummy doing here? I recall informing you not to set foot on the estate, Butterfield."

"Why's that, Red?" Antonelli beat me to the question.

"Because I'm confident Miss Fitzhugh is close to solving the crime." He narrowed his eyes at me. "It's amazing what she reveals when in certain positions."

"What did you say, Russo?" I demanded, my fingers clenching for the second time.

Smiling insincerely, Russo repeated his remark amending the last sentence to, "It's amazing what she reveals when the setting is… conducive. I am well aware how disappointing a sap you are, Butters."

"Shut up, Red." Dice Antonelli scowled. "Mr. Butterfield is a guest of our employer. If have nothing pertinent to add, go back to sniffing around that skirt you're making time with."

Both men shot me a quick look to judge my reaction; but I refused to let them rile me.

I detected the disappointment Russo tried to mask and swallowed a scornful grin.

He nodded to Antonelli and turned to leave, but I called out to stop him.

"Russo, do you stay on the estate, as well?"

"Why don't you ask Stella?" he countered with a dry chuckle and disappeared.

Antonelli glanced at me. "Anything else you need to see, Mr. Butterfield?"

"Just one last question, Mr. Antonelli. Does he have keys to the place?" I nodded in the direction Russo had taken.

"I know what you're thinking, Butterfield, but no. Like I said, there's only two sets. The boss has one and so do I."

"Okay, I'll get back to you in a couple of days."

When I returned to the office, Stella was at her desk. She eyed me coldly as I entered then dropped her gaze to the paperwork in front of her.

I poured a cup of coffee from the pot on the tabletop burner, asking, "You want a cup?"

She brandished a cup at me, "I'm good," she said without looking up.

Taking a sip, I frowned at the tepid liquid. *Thanks for letting the coffee go cold,* I groused internally. Switching on the burner, I filed some of the documents covering my desk while it heated up.

Irked by her attitude, I jumped in where angles fear to

tread. "Have you solved the case yet? Dice Antonelli showed me—"

"You were at the estate?" *That* got her attention. She raised her head to look me in the eye, her expression somewhere between disconcerted and incredulous.

"Yeah, despite *your friend's* bid to isolate me from the mansion, seems whoever pulls his strings had other ideas."

"He's not my friend, Jacob." The tell-tale flare of red washing up her cheeks belied her assertion.

"Just as Mrs. Peterson wasn't mine?" I taunted.

"Not the same."

"Semantics." I shot back, then took a deep breath. Baiting Stella would get me nowhere. I softened my tone. "Regardless, he seems to think you're close to solving the case. Is that true?"

"Possibly. I'm sure it was an inside job."

For once, in our unaccountable state of disunity, we were on the same page, and I dared pose the question, "Really? Who's your winner?" "My money's on Dice Antonelli. Something about him didn't sit right with me from the moment we were introduced."

"Of course, and I take it you noticed the absence of scoring around the locks of the door and the safe," I pressed.

"Exactly," Stella crowed triumphantly. "Plus, Dice's possession of the second set of keys makes him the obvious choice."

With no desire to get into another argument, I refrained from asking why she had not mentioned this before and threw a spanner in the works. "In that case, why did he have me kidnapped then socked me in the jaw for not coming to the estate sooner?"

"Huh?" She gaped at me.

I indicated the shiner, which she had either not noticed… although, how was beyond me… or willfully ignored.

"M-maybe, it was nothing more than a show. You know, flexing his muscles so you didn't mess with him," she hypothesized hesitantly.

"Perhaps," I conceded thoughtfully, "but, have you considered Carmine Russo?"

"R-Red?"

"It's Red now?" *Did she even register her double standards?* "Yes, Red."

"No… no, there's no way he could be involved," she defended. "I would have figured it out if that were true."

"Perhaps, if you were considering the case objectively." I challenged recklessly.

Bristling with indignation, Stella slapped her hands on the desk stood up. "I don't need to put up with this, Jacob Butterfield. You're a fine one to cast aspersions. You're trying to hurt me because you had sex with the Peterson woman and feel guilty."

"Not this again. Stella, for the last time, I did not sleep with her, and please listen to me. Russo cannot be overlo—"

"Enough. I will prove you wrong, then you and I are through."

She stormed out of the office, slamming the door behind her with such fury, the glass rattled.

I stared after her, my brain churning and my stomach knotting. In the last few hours, several pieces of the puzzle had fallen into place. I knew who had stolen the diamond, but had no proof. Just one thread, that's all I required, and the tangled web would unravel.

Needles in haystacks, Jacob, needles in haystacks.

Russo had fooled Stella but I was not so easily conned, and time was running out for me to change her mind… *and save us.*

CHAPTER TEN

I stayed at the office that night. Going home might mean encountering Stella, and I had no energy for another argument. Worse, if she was not there, I would be left with the nightmare scenario of where she was, what she was doing and, more importantly, who she was with.

I bedded down on the shabby sofa we had found on the sidewalk outside the office. The springs grumbled and squeaked as I shuffled to get comfortable and hoped to get some sleep.

Images of Red Russo lavishing Stella with gifts he had, doubtless, stolen while Stella turned a blind eye to their origin, pervaded my slumber.

Eventually, in spite of the tempest reverberating around my brain, I dozed off in the middle of the night… sometime after the third police siren sped by and faded into the distance… or was that also my imagination?

I was dreaming about an annoying woodpecker destroying a rotting oak tree when my subconscious suggested it was probably someone knocking on the door and exhorted me to wake up. With effort I followed the instruction, to be dazzled by the early morning sun.

Blinking until the dancing dots dissipated, I stared at the door, discerning the shadow of a woman through the glass. My brain tried to convince me it was Stella, but logic informed me my visitor was too small to be my partner.

Why would Stella bother knocking?

Another, more insistent, rap.

"Yeah, yeah, hold your goddamned horses," I groused, forcing my aching body off the sofa. Stifling a yawn, I stretched the painful kinks out of my spine.

Looking as disheveled as a waterfront lush, I turned the key, and swung open the door. "The door was locked, that usually infers a business is closed."

A mouse of a woman looked up at me, eyes wide with fright. "I-Is Miss Fitzhugh in? S-She told me to come to her office immed—"

"*Her* office?" I sniped.

"This is her place of work, yes?"

"For the time being, but she's not here right now." I took a step back. "Why don't you come in and explain it to me?"

She gave me a wary look and refused to move. Stella's… informant… I had to suppose, appeared to be judging me by my wrinkled suit and scruffy hair.

Sighing, I clarified, "I am Jacob Butterfield, proprietor of this agency. It is safe to tell me whatever you were going to tell Miss Fitzhugh."

I watched her pluck up the courage to enter, and her voice wavered as she replied, "My name is Ida Weaver. I am one of the maids working for Mister Lan— I mean the estate, where Miss Fitzhugh has been investigating. She asked me to come here if I discovered anything which might be significant."

I ushered her to the nearest wingback chair, deposited her in it, perhaps less than gently, and headed for some much-needed morning joe.

Lifting the pot from the hot plate, I offered, "Would you care for a cup?" at the same moment as I lifted the lid to see the tar remnants from last night. *Just great.*

Replacing the ruined pot, I improvised brightly, "Gin and tonic?"

"At this time of the day? I should say not. I'm not sure what sort of woman you think I am, Mister Butterfield, but I work as a domestic help—"

"Okay, okay. Point taken. No alcohol for you. It's just the coffee..." I gestured at the pot morosely, then pulled myself together. "Now, tell me what bothers you?"

Her reproach evaporated. "I-I think Mister Russo murdered Mister Antonelli."

It was my turn to give the hairy eye. "Could you repeat that please?"

"Last night, I was heading to Mister Russo's room—"

My arched brow stopped her dead in her tracks, and earned me a, "Don't be disgusting."

I extended my hand apologetically, inviting her to continue.

"As I was saying, I was going to Mister Russo's room because a couple of weeks ago, he asked me to add an..." frowning, she hesitated, and I could practically see the wheels spinning in her head. "Infusion, that's it, he called it an infusion, to Mister Antonelli's scotch, which I always served when they played cards. He promised to give me a little extra for my help but had forgotten." Her dry tone implying this was not unusual.

"When was this?" I jotted down the information, my detective senses on high alert.

"U-umm the night they think that diamond went missing."

"Why didn't you tell anyone about it at the time?"

"Never thought about it then. I didn't connect the two things. I've been working there a long time and did question him about the..." she faltered.

"Infusion," I supplied helpfully. She glowered at me.

"Yes, but Mister Russo said it was something the Irish were developing to enrich the flavor of cheap alcohol. I must say that confused me because our employer stocks only the expensive stuff.

"Anyway, I did as I was told and made sure Mister Antonelli got the scotch. Mister Russo had a vodka tonic," she clarified, which saved me asking how she knew whose drink was whose, but also reminded me that Russo had ordered a highball at the Kings Swan Inn. *Interesting*.

"Middle of the evening, Mister Antonelli complained about feeling groggy, and Mister Russo insisted on helping him to bed."

"How do you know this?" I felt the hairs on the back of my neck prickle.

"I'm always hand in case they want anything during their games. Drinks or food," she replied as though that was obvious. "Same every night they play cards."

I nodded my understanding. "So, because Mister Antonelli was taken ill, you assumed Mister Russo would pay you later and he didn't?"

She sucked on her top lip before answering, "Exactly. I have bills like the next person, and every little extra helps." She tried to justify her actions, but her awkward fidgeting told me she felt guilty for following Russo's instructions.

I almost felt sorry for her. Her hands were tied. Do as

you're told or lose your job. Ida was just following orders. *How many times has that led people down the wrong path?*

I coaxed my weary brain back to the moment, to hear her say, "I just wanted to jog his memory, which was why I went to see him last night."

"And you witnessed Russo killing Antonelli?" Given she was still alive, this was improbable, but I had to ask.

"Gracious me, no. I was about to knock on the door when I heard them yelling at each other. Mr. Antonelli accused Mr. Russo of drugging him and stealing the keys to the boss's office. I think they were having a bit of a fist fight, because there were loud grunts and a lot of cursing. Oh, their language."

She paused, blatantly appalled, and I had bite my lip to smother an ill-timed laugh at her consternation, surmising Miss Weaver would not appreciate my sense of humour.

Gathering herself, she continued, "Then there was a muffled bang."

"What did you do?"

"Me? I ducked around the corner at the end of the hall. Just in time too, the door opened, and Mr. Russo peered out to see if anyone was there."

"I'm amazed he didn't see you," I could not prevent the hint of scepticism creeping into my voice.

"I hid until the door closed."

"Then how did you know it was Mr. Russo and not Mr. Antonelli who looked out?" A valid and rather important question.

"I heard him muttering to himself. There's no mistaking his voice for Mr. Antonelli's. I tell ya, my blood ran cold." Ida shuddered. "Then I hightailed it out of there."

"Probably a good job you didn't hang around. Might not have ended well," I remarked… pointlessly, while cheering inwardly. I had my thread.

"Ya think?" Ida snorted. "Instead of stating the obvious, how about giving me some advice… or…" she let that dangle, and it did not take a genius to figure out her inference.

Hanging on one wall of the office was a portrait of Honest Abe. I lifted it down to expose a safe. Twisting the dial, I popped it open and reached in to pluck out a couple of bills from the small stash.

I handed them to Ida. "Take these and make yourself scarce but let me know where to find you," I said as I closed and secured the safe. Taking advantage of my momentary inattention, Miss Weaver, without so much as a thank you, fled in a staccato rat-a-tat of heels. The office door crashed back into its frame with such vehemence, I expected the glass to shatter. *Honestly, these women and their dramatic exits.*

"Shit," I hissed, annoyed with myself. I detest being taken for a soft touch. "Fool you once, Butters," I growled balefully.

The loss of twenty dollars was the least of my worries. I could always charge that to my mysterious employer. No, my major concern circled the fact, Stella Fitzhugh, the woman I could no longer deny I needed in my life, was flirting with a thief and murderer.

Sometimes, I hate being right.

Snatching the file off the desk, I grabbed my hat and headed out to the only place I could think of where I might find the recently elusive Stella Fitzhugh.

I reached my apartment building and, leaving the file in the car for now, sprinted up the stairs two at a time, barely catching my landlady's bleated complaint that this was a reputable residence, not the local brothel.

"You tell that young woman of yours," her gravelly, cigarette-roughened voice followed my ascent.

"Whatever," I called over my shoulder in what I hoped were conciliatory tones.

Bursting through my door, I was met with dead air and a sense of emptiness.

Stella had gone, along with all her things.

Not quite empty.

The distinctive click of a pistol's hammer engaging reached my ears, accompanied by a deep-throated chuckle as the apartment door closed with an ominous thunk.

Instinctively, I went for my gun ready to face the intruder to be halted by a familiar voice.

"Not so fast, Butterfield. Drop the hog first. Then turn around, slowly and carefully."

Carmine 'Red' Russo.

Discretion being the better part of valor — I was no use to Stella dead — I did as instructed. Suited up, as though on the way to the theater, Russo was lounging against the wall behind the door, invisible until I had stepped right inside the apartment.

The split second during which I contemplated how long he had been waiting for me, was superseded immediately by a more pressing matter… in the form of a .45 pointed at my chest.

I met his arrogant gaze without flinching, itching to wipe the insolent smirk off his mouth and beat him to a bloody pulp.

"By your hasty entrance, might I be correct in deducing you hoped to find someone else? Oh dear, I am sorry to be the bearer of bad news, but Miss Fitzhugh is finished with you and has decided a change of scenery is in order, with benefits, of course."

"You bastard," I snarled, daring to take a step closer.

"Uh oh, big boy, do not tempt me."

"I won't let you steal Stella like you did the diamond."

"Come now, Butterfield, you lost your partner way before I showed up. Sadly, you were too blind and inept to realize it. As for the diamond, I didn't steal it, Dice did."

"Bullshit. You stole it and framed Antonelli, then murdered him so he couldn't defend himself."

"Well, well, well. Credit where credit's due, maybe I was hasty in my judgement of your skill as PI. Unfortunately, Dice paid for his sins, and for being gullible enough to trust me. When I returned the rock to my employer, he was most appreciative and thanked me for my diligence. Regrettably, that means you forgo the finder's fee, I promised. Entirely your own fault for dragging your heels in the investigation."

Desperate to teach Mr Carmine Russo a long overdue lesson, my fingers clenched into a ball, and I gritted my teeth.

He didn't seem to notice, and carried on, his oily tone grating on me. "As for me, the reward for proving my worth to the boss is a promotion. I am going to Vegas to oversee his property investments."

"What's with the confession, Russo? Do you intend to kill me?"

Straightening up, he laughed, "Hardly, that would be too quick and painless. My plan is to inflict an excruciating and prolonged torture."

Before I could blink, never mind duck, Russo had flipped the pistol in his hand, and smashed the grip against my temple. Stars exploded in front of my eyes, and my knees buckled.

Russo bent close, gave a humorless laugh, and sneered, "I'm gonna let you spend the rest of your miserable life knowing the dame is mine!"

Then everything went black.

FINALE

I became aware of a dull pounding in my brain. Groggily, I peeled back my eyelids, squinting in the glare of the sun streaming through the window.

Flat on my back, I felt the cold wood of the floor seeping through my clothes, prompting me to shift, and I fought the urge to scream when my muscles protested the sudden movement.

What the fuck?

Recollection hovered and splintered, then coalesced. *Stella.*

Ignoring my spinning head, I struggled to my feet and gripped the back of the chair to steady myself. *Stella.* I had to get to her, warn her, declare my love for her… whatever it took to get her back.

I splashed cold water on my face, trying to corral my thoughts, filtering through the trivial to get to the relevant.

He was going to Vegas.

Stella wanted a change of scene.

He was taking her with him.

I had yet to fathom what it was about Russo that Stella found attractive. Two weeks. *Two weeks*! Not even that... closer to one.

He was older than her by a good decade, possibly two, heavyset, a polite term for rotund, too smarmy by half, and a face even his own mother would struggle to call handsome. Yeah, yeah, while his features did not equate to his character, I knew Stella. She was not shallow, but looks were important to her, and Russo was no oil painting... unknowingly echoing my partner's initial opinion of the man.

Ok, I had my faults, but I thought we had something special. That it had become more than just sex, although that was always passionate. A shared history if nothing else. We created the agency together, built up a reputation as generally decent — if occasionally, morally gray — investigators, and were growing steadily.

Clearly, I was mistaken.

Was I about to let her go without a fight?

Hell no!

My thoughts screeched to a halt. Vegas. Train or car?

By car, there were too many variables until I got out of the city onto the highway, but the train? I mulled over the likelihood of both and decided the train was the most probable... should one be running today, which, given Russo's cocky behavior, was a reasonable bet. Still an interminable journey with at least one transfer, but easier and relatively more luxurious.

An egomaniac, Russo wanted nothing more than to win, and first class tickets were a sure fire way to impress Stella, increasing his standing in her eyes and, by extension, his influence over her. I am not unaware of the, apparently, magical properties of money, recalling more than one occasion when Stella alleged I must be related to Scrooge.

I pulled on a clean shirt, if I had *any* chance of winning my fair lady, I needed to look like I gave a damn, and hurtled down the stairs to the car.

I drove like a bat out of hell to the station, my mind churning. How to persuade Stella that my love was genuine, that any dereliction of devotion was inadvertent and would never *ever* be repeated.

All the way to the station, I rehearsed what I believed to be an evidence-based, articulate, and incontrovertible argument to convince Stella that she and I were a match made in heaven… or, at least, California.

Assuming, of course, I could persuade her to listen.

Surely, she would listen…

I pressed my foot on the gas pedal, trying to quash my rapidly escalating panic that I might miss the train.

I parked or rather abandoned the car at the Southern Pacific Depot on Third and Townsend, and ran full pelt into the ticket hall to scour the board for the Coast Line platform. Much as I appreciated the elegant interior, light spilling through its huge arched windows to illuminate the soft sheen of the wooden benches and the tiled floor, today I was not interested in admiring the architecture.

The train was due to depart. I had mere minutes.

Like a man possessed, I sprinted onto the platform. Hunkered down on the rails, the great machine belched smoke as passengers embarked, while people milled about shouting their farewells.

I hurried along the train, checking every window. *Where was she?*

The whistle blew…

Nooooo...

Then I spotted her.

Dressed like a fashion model, her hair perfectly coiffured

under a jaunty hat, Stella was leaning on the open window but looking at someone inside the compartment.

"Stella," I bellowed.

She twisted to face my direction, her expression morphing from cheerful to startled.

I watched her mouth form the word, "Butters?"

I reached her just as the train started to move. It was now or never.

"Don't go. He doesn't deserve you."

"Butters, what is this? You know we are over. I need to be the most important thing in your life. I can't accept anything less."

The engine chugged. The wheels turned, grinding as they hauled the sinuous line of shining carriages.

"Stella, give me another chance." I hated the plea in my voice, but I had nothing to lose.

She leaned out and her fingers grazed my cheek. "Too late, Jacob. Red can give me the world, and he wants to marry me. You barely noticed my existence."

"Hey, not true." I was panting now, and the platform was running out. "Never mind me, you need to know something about Russo…"

"Too late, Jacob," she said sadly. "You are far too late."

The train gathered speed.

Stella waved. "Goodbye Butters, it was fun while it lasted."

I managed to stop my headlong dash before I fell onto the tracks.

The 3:15 to Los Angeles gained momentum and was soon little more than a mirage in the afternoon haze. I stood motionless, my gaze fixed on the locomotive until it disappeared.

Ignoring the quizzical faces of those who had witnessed

my humiliation, I trudged back to the ticket hall and out to my car, which, miraculously, had avoided a ticket.

Despondently, I climbed in and sat, drumming my fingers on the steering wheel. *What on earth was I supposed to do now?*

A reluctant chuckle escaped my lips, and I shook my head.

Perhaps I ought to report a murder.

SIBLING RIVALRY
Butters P.I.

CHAPTER ONE

1942 - San Francisco

June 1942. Not only was America hip deep in a war which encompassed half the planet, but also, and more fortuitously, had won a major battle in the Pacific at Midway against the Japanese Imperial Navy.

In the months leading up to the victory, troops were moved in and out of San Francisco on their way to Pearl Harbor, Hawaii, and points west.

'Frisco had, for want of a better description, become the Grand Central Station for the US military, their numbers almost, but not quite, overshadowing the disparate quota of unsavory characters lurking on the fringes of the city, whose intent was far less… laudable.

The waterfront was rife with gangsters, spies, and small-time criminals, intent on making the most out of skimming war materials and cashing in on humanity's confusion.

As for me… none of that mattered.

I flipped through my paper, remembering cheery days spent in a muddy trench during the last war, before returning to my beloved City by the Bay, where I was a detective for ten years.

A flourishing career arrested, to coin a phrase, when the SFPD became mired in allegations of graft and corruption… more specifically, yours truly… none of which were proved by the way. Regrettably, my claims of innocence were ignored. As far as the brass was concerned, they had their scapegoat.

My stroll down memory lane was interrupted by a sharp rap on my door. A shapely silhouette through the frosted glass announced my next prospective client was waiting to be invited in.

"Come in." *No one pays me to be a doorman.*

The door swung open to reveal a beautiful, bleached blonde. Without so much as a *Hello, Detective, my life is in danger,* she sashayed into my office and settled in the chair at the opposite side of my desk.

Removing a cigarette from a sterling silver case, she tapped the end on the metal, packing the tobacco tightly like a pro, and slipped it between her Hollywood-starlet red lips.

She sat there without a word, her fingers tapping on the arm of the chair impatiently. Apparently, my visitor expected me to get off my ass to light her smoke.

At first, I considered exercising my ego and telling her there was no smoking in my office but her baby-blues were too enticing to ignore. So, I took the bait.

Rounding the cluttered desk, I rifled in my pocket for my lighter. Standing in front of her, I snapped it open casually, hitting that one-in-a-million chance of it coming to life instantly. I leaned against the edge of the desk and offered her a light.

"Ya know, doll, I don't let just anyone smoke in my place," I remonstrated, keeping my tone mild.

"Does that make me special?" She arched a cool brow, the faintest hint of a condescending smile curving her mouth.

"No, being a Wentworth does that," I replied in kind. "To what do I owe the pleasure of a visit from one of the city's elite?"

At this, her coy composure crumbled. An ugly wrinkle furrowed her forehead, distorting her beautiful face.

"Mr. Butter, my sister has been—" she began.

"It's Butterfield," I corrected.

"Excuse me?"

"The name is Jacob Butterfield."

"But the name on your door—"

"A souvenir from a disgruntled and incompetent door artist. It serves as an ironic reminder that a finished job, no matter the outcome, is better than not getting it done at all."

My potential client smirked. "In other words, you're too cheap to have it redone?"

"Let's just say frugal."

There was no sense explaining that, as a result, everyone in the Greater San Francisco Area referring to me as Butters. To change it now, would be like changing who I am... and, yes, I'm too cheap.

"Given you obviously didn't look me up in the phonebook, how about you tell me how you found my place, and why?"

"Mr. Butterfield, I'm terribly anxious about my younger sister, Pamela. She was supposed to meet her boyfriend at some seedy gin joint on the Waterfront two days ago, and I haven't heard from her since.

"I fear she may have fallen into trouble."

This didn't answer my question, but I returned to my side of the desk and dug a semi-crushed pack of smokes out of the suit coat draped over the back of my chair. Sliding one out, I clenched it between my lips and lit it.

I let the cloud of smoke billow around me then asked, "How do I fit into your game of Hide and Seek?"

"I asked around the docks whether there was a private investigator trustworthy enough to find her," the elder Miss Wentworth went on, not sparing the charm.

"Okay, Miss Wentworth, skip the fairytale and tell me the truth."

I suspected she thought I was another uneducated gorilla who could not read, much like the muscled suit photographed trailing behind her when she left the Federal Court House.

A photograph which was splashed across every major newspaper in the country, along with the accompanying tale of woe between Vanessa and Pamela Wentworth.

It was also no secret the sisters bore no love for each other, thanks, in part, to the multimillion-dollar inheritance their late father had left them…and the fact they had different mothers.

Vanessa, the only child of their father's first marriage, was left motherless at the age of eight. The younger daughter, Pamela, was the result of a tryst with a maid no longer in the picture.

If the gossip columns were to be believed — and I never missed a single issue because that was where the juiciest details could be found — Pamela had reached the stage where she wanted to live her entire life in one day. Parties, new men, spending money like water.

All that came to an end when, in the old man's haste to check out of this world, he neglected to specify in his will *how* the money was to be divided, tying up the funds in probate.

Adding insult to injury, as always seemed to be the case in these messy situations, a mysterious second will materialize, leaving everything to the older daughter should the younger be proved mentally unstable, and Pamela had done a sterling job to earn that diagnosis.

The press was having a field day with the animosity between the siblings.

Taking a drag on her cigarette, the end burning as red-hot as the glare she gave me, Vanessa let the smoke roll out of her mouth with a huff.

"Fine, long story short, I need you to find her. Hopefully in one piece."

"Why don't you just go to the police? Missing people fall under their jurisdiction."

"Because if she turns up dead, I'll be the only suspect."

"Point taken. I'm sure my fee of fifty dollars a day, plus expenses, won't be a problem?" I observed politely.

"Find her in one piece and I'll double it."

Ignoring all rational arguments to the contrary, I took a leap of faith, unable to decide whether I wanted Vanessa where I could keep an eye on her or for other, less… gallant reasons. "For the time being, why don't you hide yourself at my place? It's not much, but neither is it crawling with cops, or bad guys."

Vanessa studied her surroundings suspiciously.

I chuckled, "Doll, I'd never think of keeping you here. I have an even seedier place in mind, but I can guarantee no one will find you there.

Reluctantly, she agreed.

RORI BLEU

With a smattering of riverboat pirates and royalty in her heritage, Rori Bleu's childhood reflected her past.
An interest in fairy tales, myth and legend were as important as spirited discussions around politics and current affairs — although some might argue they are one and the same!

A fascination, sparked by listening to Grimm's Fairy Tales at her grandmother's knee, not only encouraged Rori's passion for reading, but also steered her into the world of RPG's. What began as a fun pastime, soon evolved into the creation of fantastical worlds, but Rori never lost her love of politics going on to specialise in Governmental History and Historical Research.

Naturally this means her stories are steeped in historical accuracy and real-life intrigue. While Rori's love of a happily ever after means her preferred genre is romance, don't be surprised if you discover an occasional detour into historical fiction, thrillers, horror and fantasy.

ALSO BY RORI BLEU

Pineapple Meringue

Imprisoned Hearts

Port of London

Dani's Masquerade

Black Tulips

Ajei's Destiny

Porta Aeternum

The Queen's Heart

Syn *with Matthew Forester*

With Rosie Chapel

Tapestry of Shadows and Light - The Hunters Prequel

Echoes and Illusions - The Hunters: Book 1

Smoke and Mirrors - The Hunters : Book 2

Evie's War

Vindicta

Corrupt Covenant

Lesser of Two Evils

Deadly Incision

Tidbits

The Sela Helsdatter Saga

A Flip of The Coin - Book One

Conceived Chaos - Book Two

Odin's Bane - Book Three

Valhalla's Doom - Book Four

Arcane Alchemy: Freya's Fate - *A Helsdatter Saga Novella*

P.I. Butters Series

Double Cross

Dereliction of Devotion

Sibling Rivalry

The Mobster's Moll

ALSO BY ROSIE CHAPEL

<u>Historical Fiction</u>

The Hannah's Heirloom Sequence
The Pomegranate Tree - Book One
Echoes of Stone and Fire - Book Two
Embers of Destiny - Book Three
Etched in Starlight - Prequel
Hannah's Heirloom Trilogy - Compilation — e-book only

Prelude to Fate
Legacy of Flame and Ash

The Nettleby Trilogy (WW1 Novellas)
A Guardian Unexpected - Book One
Under the Clock - Book Two
Between Heartbeats - Book Three

<u>Regency Romances</u>
The Linen and Lace Series
Once Upon An Earl - Book One
To Unlock Her Heart - Book Two
Love on a Winter's Tide - Book Three
A Love Unquenchable - Book Four
A Hidden Rose — Book Five

An Unexpected Romance
Elusive Hearts - Book One

Shrouded Hearts - Book Two

The Daffodil Garden

The Unconventional Duchess

Rescuing Her Knight - *the de Wiltons:* Book One

His Fiery Hoyden

A Regency Duet

A Regency Christmas Double

Fate is Curious

A Christmas Prayer *with Ashlee Shades*

The Lady's Wager

Winning Emma

A Love Impossible

Unravelling Roana

Love Kindled

Moonbeams and Mistletoe

The Baron's Inheritance

<u>airy Tale Romance</u>
Chasing Bluebells

<u>Contemporary Romances</u>
Of Ruins and Romance

All At Once It's You

Cobweb Dreams

Just One Step

His Heart's Second Sigh